THE BATMAN STRIKES!®

Raintree

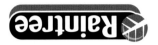

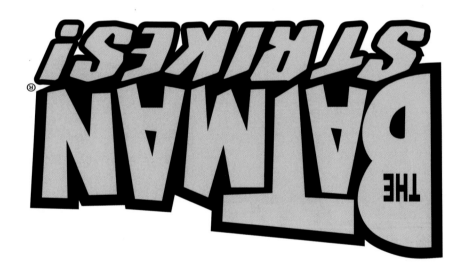

THE BATMAN STRIKES!®

Raintree is an imprint of Capstone Global Library Limited, a company incorporated in England and Wales having its registered office at 7 Pilgrim Street, London, EC4V 6LB - Registered company number: 6695582

First published by Raintree in 2014
The moral rights of the proprietor have been asserted.

Originally published by DC Comics in the US in single magazine form as The Batman Strikes! #2.

Ashley C. Andersen Zantop *Publisher*
Michael Dahl *Editorial Director*
Sean Tulien *Editor*
Heather Kindseth *Creative Director*
Bob Lentz *Designer*
Kathy McColley *Production Specialist*

DC COMICS
Joan Hilty & Harvey Richards *Original U.S. Editors*
Jeff Matsuda & Dave McCaig *Cover Artists*

ISBN 978 1 406 27962 7

Printed in China by Nordica
1013/CA21301918
17 16 15 14 13
10 9 8 7 6 5 4 3 2 1

British Library Cataloguing in Publication Data
A full catalogue record for this book is available from the British Library.

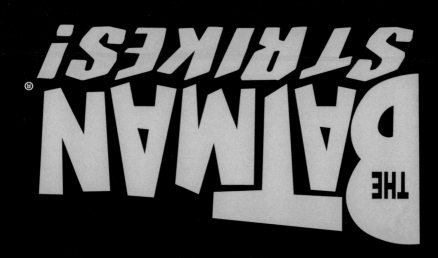

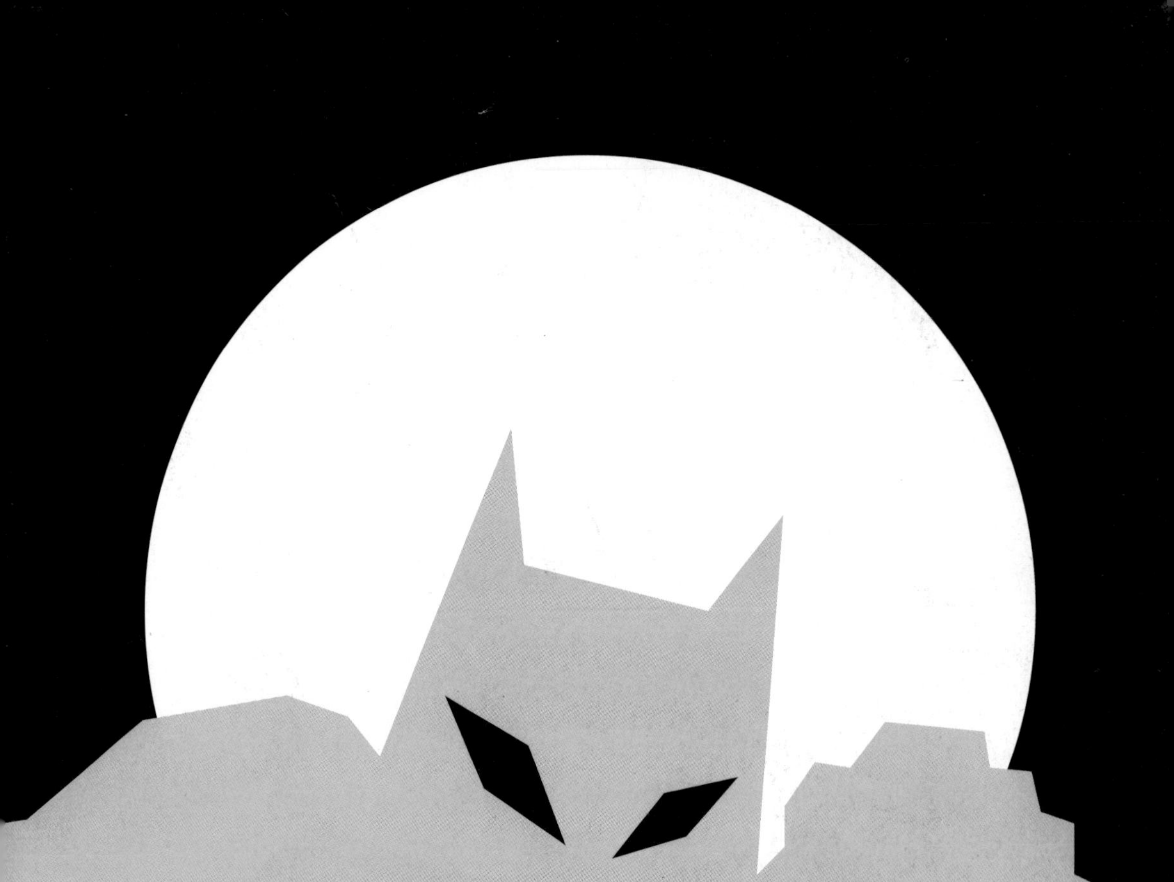

GOING... BATTY!

BILL MATHENY ....WRITER
CHRISTOPHER JONES ....PENCILLER
TERRY BEATTY.......................INKER
HEROIC AGE....................COLOURIST
NICK J. NAPOLITANO...........LETTERER

BATMAN CREATED BY
BOB KANE

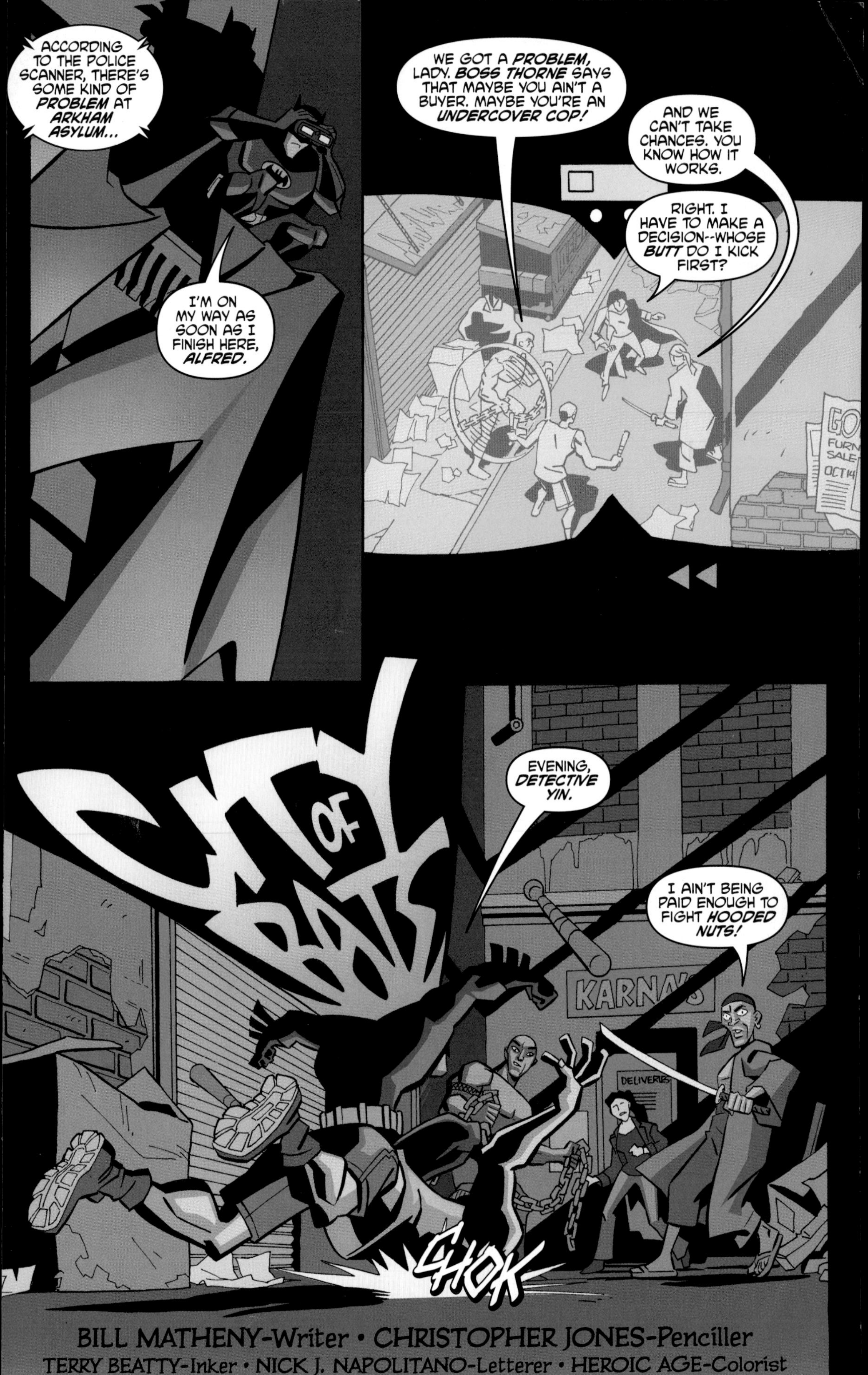
ACCORDING TO THE POLICE SCANNER, THERE'S SOME KIND OF *PROBLEM* AT *ARKHAM ASYLUM...*
I'M ON MY WAY AS SOON AS I FINISH HERE, *ALFRED.*
WE GOT A *PROBLEM,* LADY. *BOSS THORNE* SAYS THAT MAYBE YOU AIN'T A BUYER. MAYBE YOU'RE AN *UNDERCOVER COP!*
AND WE CAN'T TAKE CHANCES. YOU KNOW HOW IT WORKS.
RIGHT. I HAVE TO MAKE A DECISION--WHOSE *BUTT* DO I KICK FIRST?
GO
FURN
SALE
OCT 14
CITY OF BATS
EVENING, *DETECTIVE YIN.*
I AIN'T BEING PAID ENOUGH TO FIGHT *HOODED NUTS!*
KARNA'S
DELIVERIES
CHOK

BILL MATHENY-Writer • CHRISTOPHER JONES-Penciller
TERRY BEATTY-Inker • NICK J. NAPOLITANO-Letterer • HEROIC AGE-Colorist
HARVEY RICHARDS-Asst Editor • JOAN HILTY-editor • BATMAN created by BOB KANE

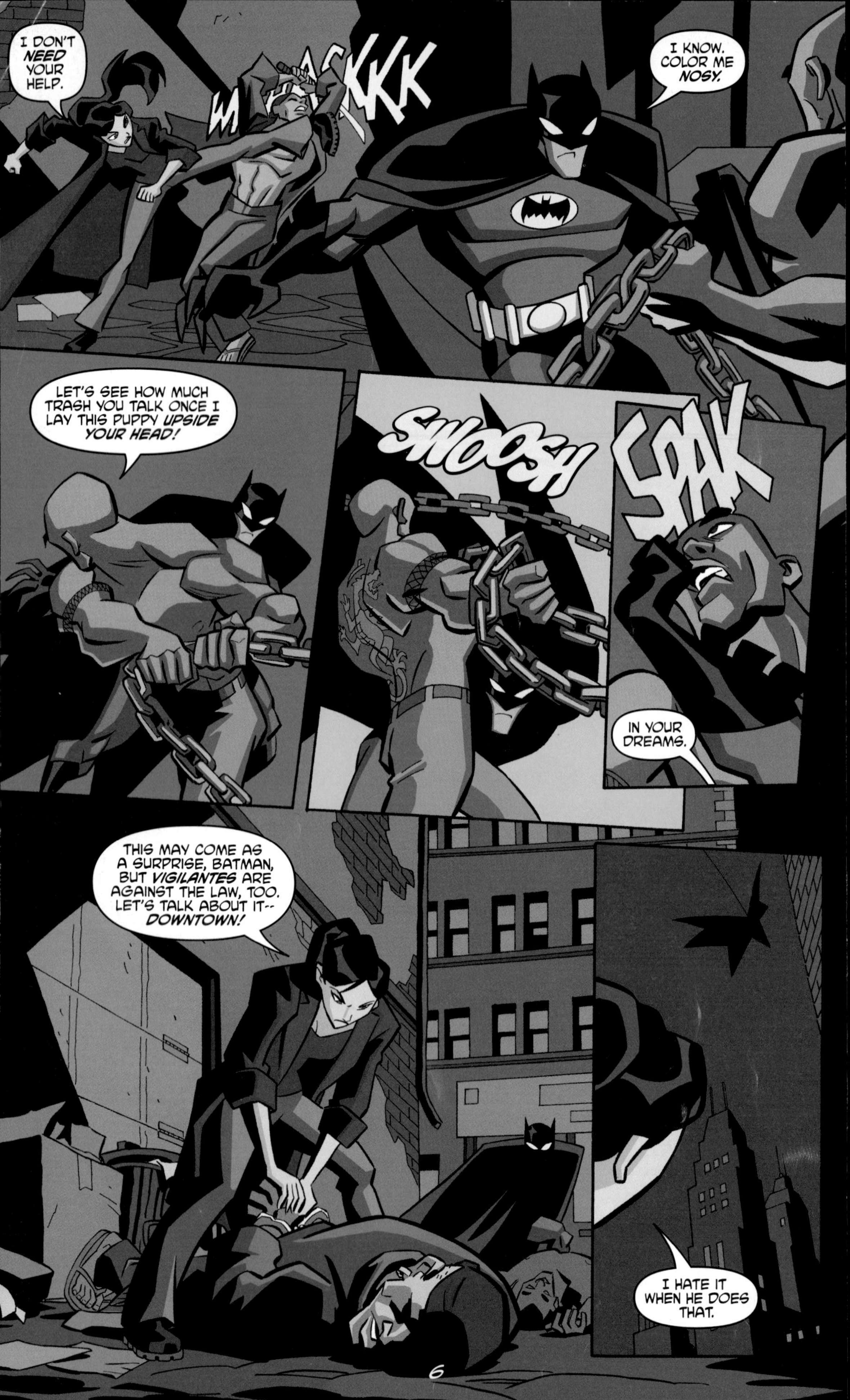
I DON'T *NEED* YOUR HELP.
I KNOW. COLOR ME *NOSY.*
LET'S SEE HOW MUCH TRASH YOU TALK ONCE I LAY THIS PUPPY *UPSIDE YOUR HEAD!*
SWOOSH
SPAK
IN YOUR DREAMS.
THIS MAY COME AS A SURPRISE, BATMAN, BUT *VIGILANTES* ARE AGAINST THE LAW, TOO. LET'S TALK ABOUT IT-- *DOWNTOWN!*
I HATE IT WHEN HE DOES THAT.

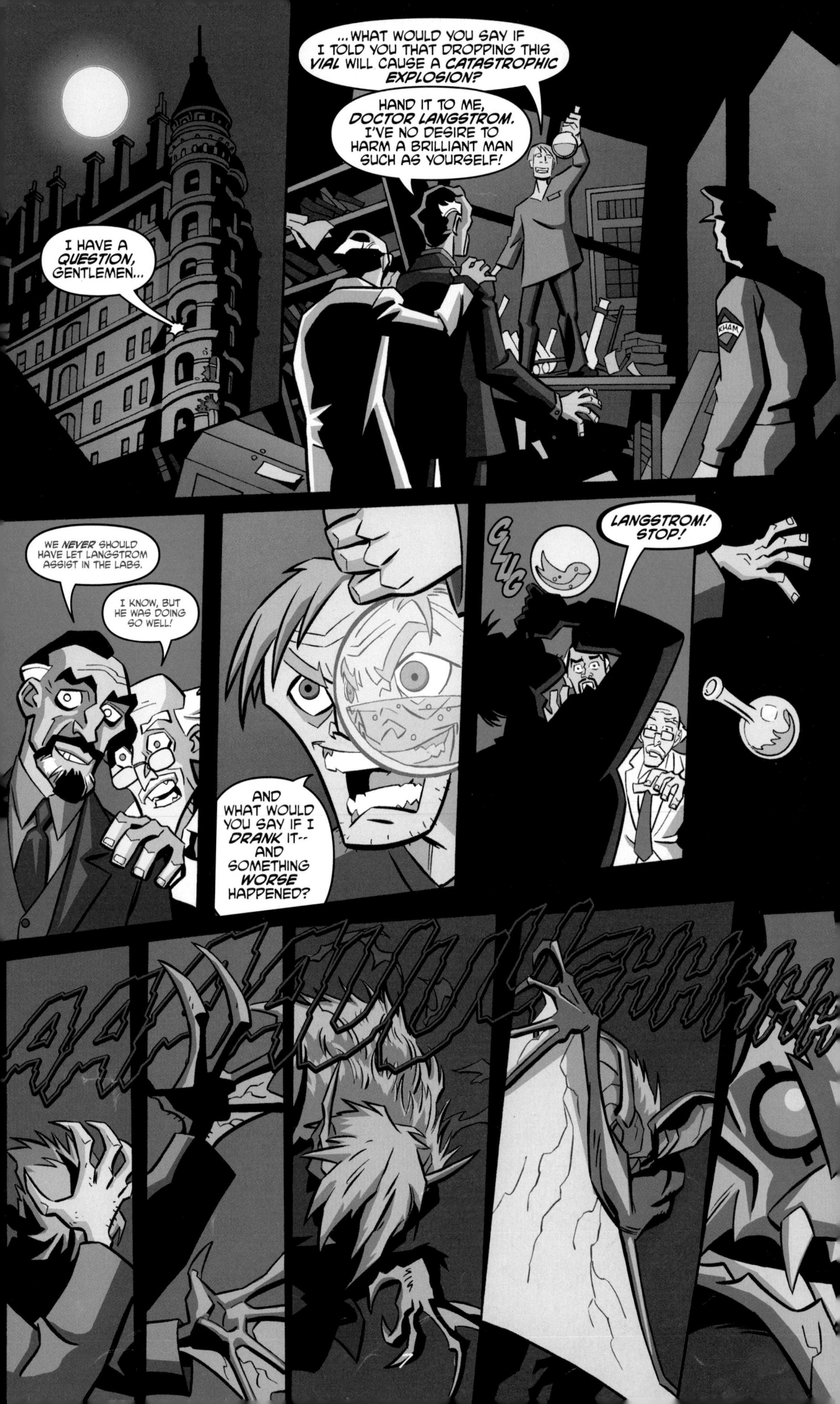
I HAVE A QUESTION, GENTLEMEN...
...WHAT WOULD YOU SAY IF I TOLD YOU THAT DROPPING THIS VIAL WILL CAUSE A CATASTROPHIC EXPLOSION?
HAND IT TO ME, DOCTOR LANGSTROM. I'VE NO DESIRE TO HARM A BRILLIANT MAN SUCH AS YOURSELF!
KHAM
WE NEVER SHOULD HAVE LET LANGSTROM ASSIST IN THE LABS.
I KNOW, BUT HE WAS DOING SO WELL!
AND WHAT WOULD YOU SAY IF I DRANK IT-- AND SOMETHING WORSE HAPPENED?
GLUG
LANGSTROM! STOP!
AAAAUUUUGHHHHHH

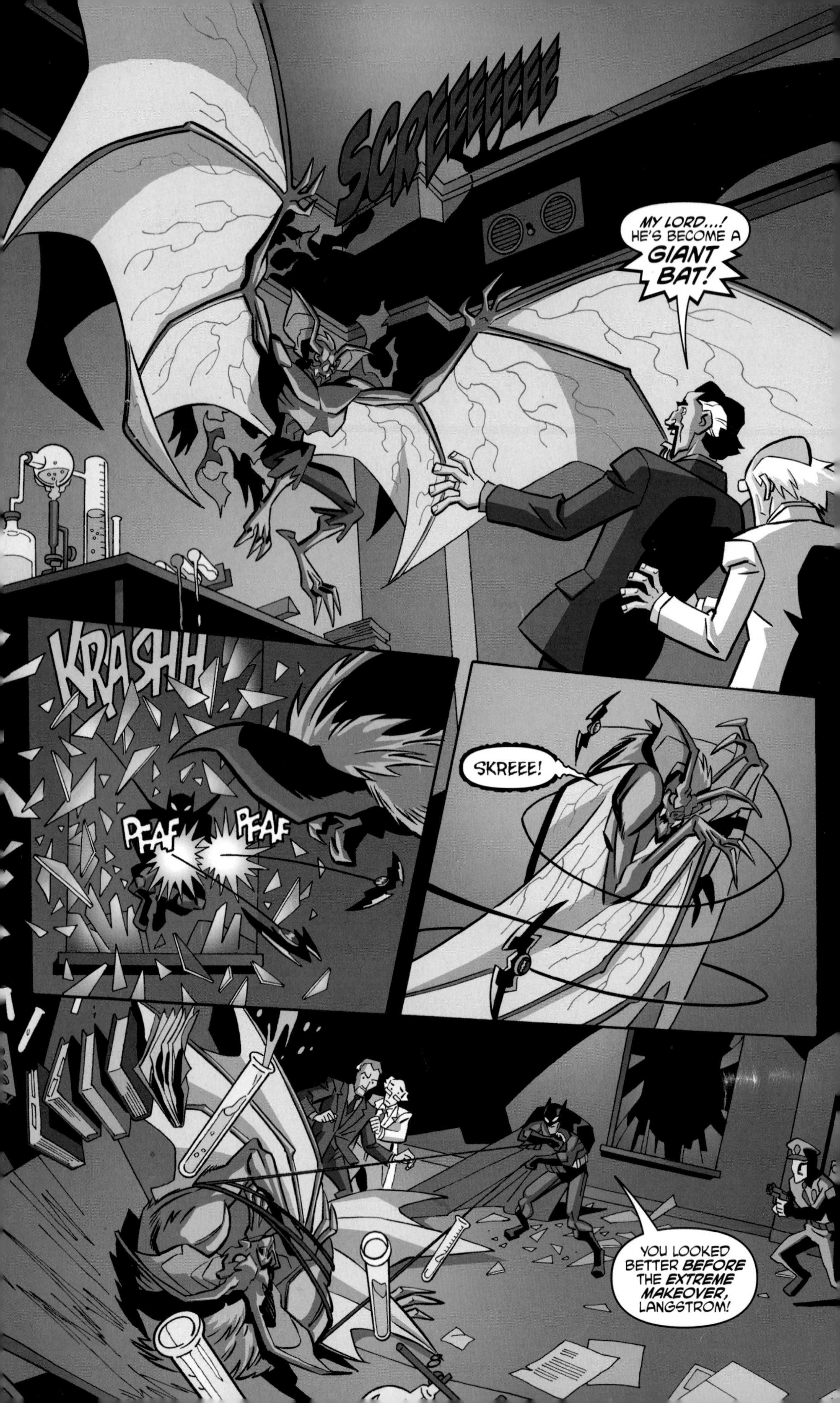
SCREEEEEEE
MY LORD...! HE'S BECOME A GIANT BAT!
KRASHH
PFAF
PFAF
SKREEE!
YOU LOOKED BETTER BEFORE THE EXTREME MAKEOVER, LANGSTROM!

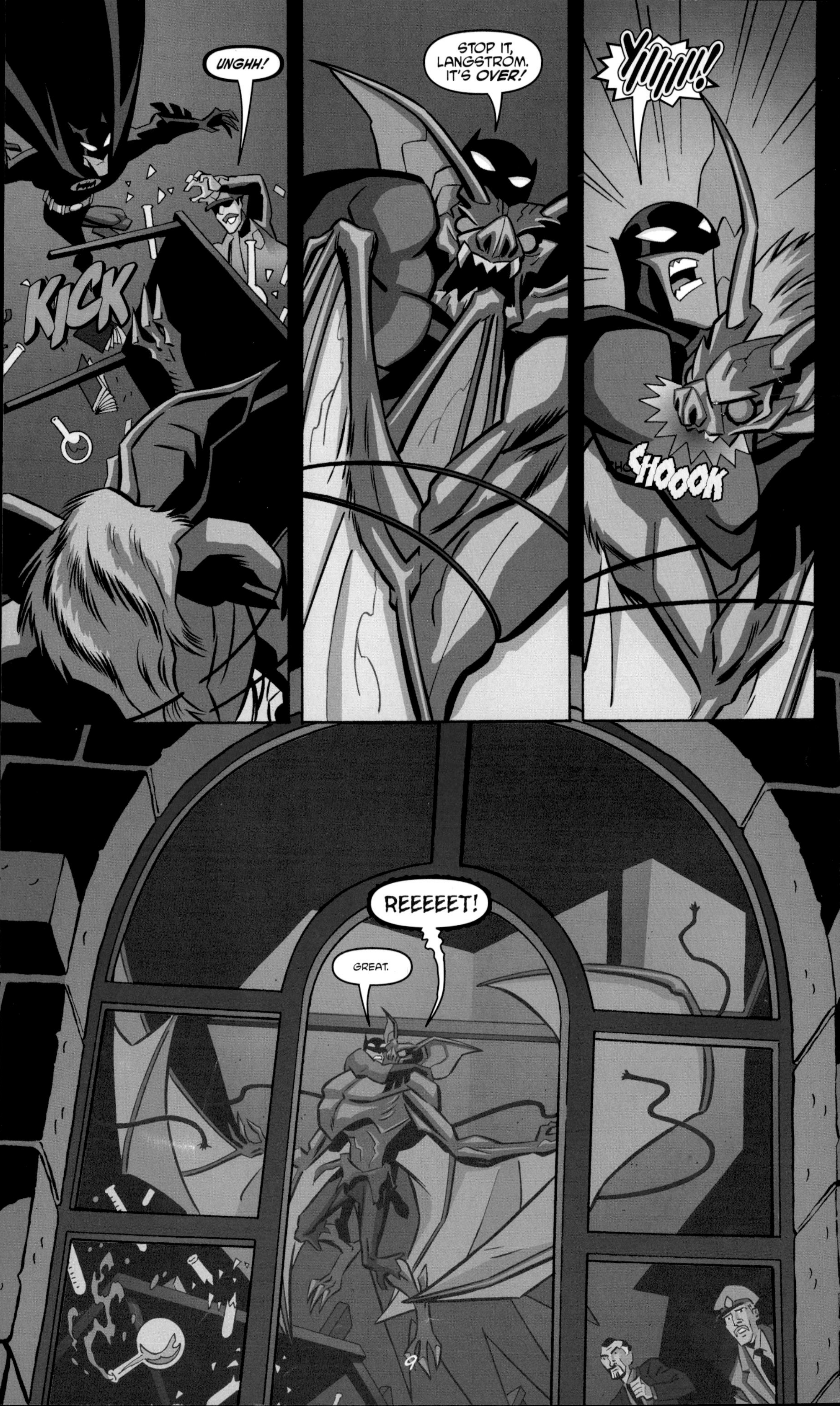
UNGHH!
KICK
STOP IT, LANGSTROM. IT'S OVER!
YIIIII!
CHOOOK
REEEEET!
GREAT.

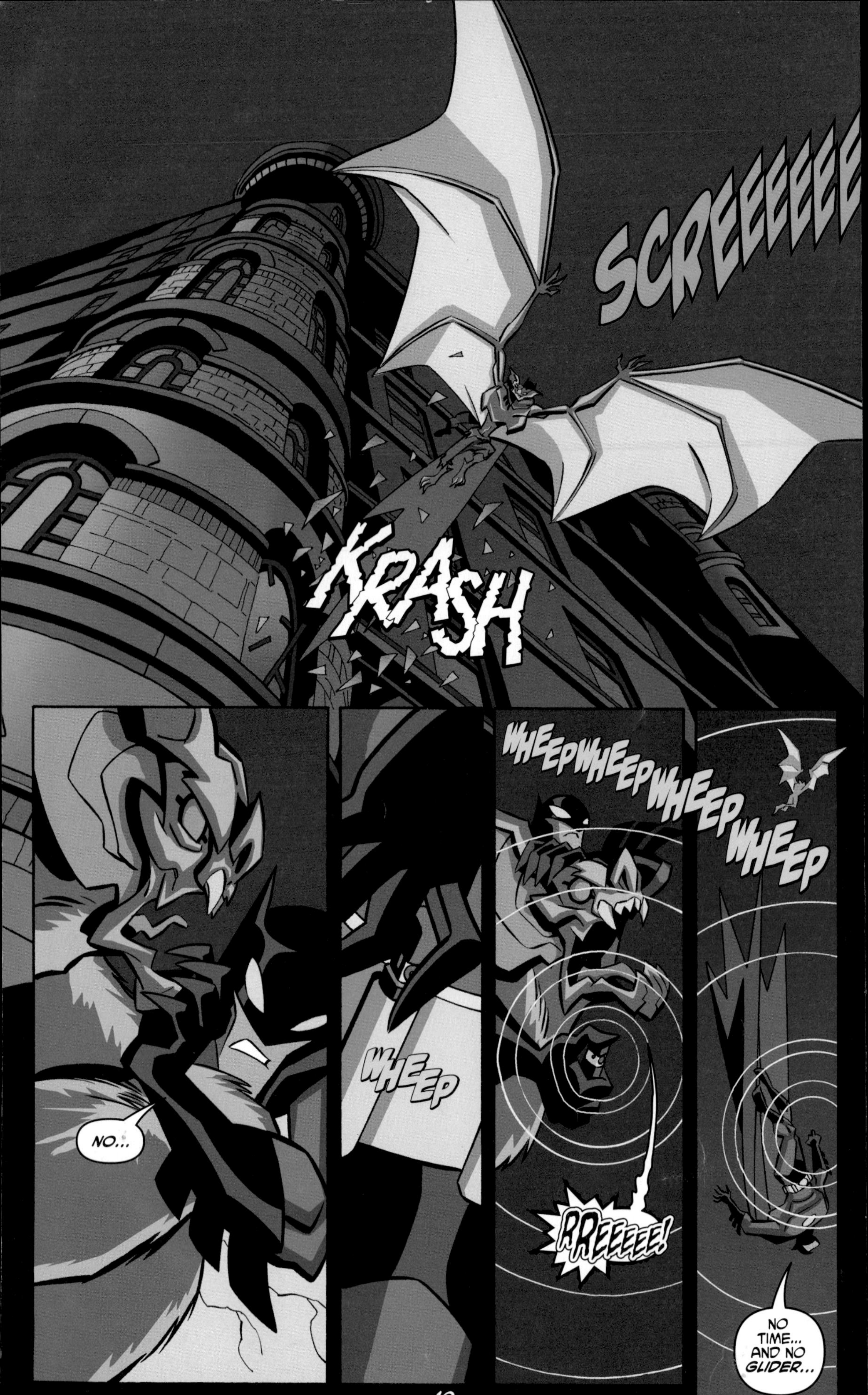
SCREEEEEE
KRASH
NO...
WHEEP
WHEEPWHEEPWHEEPWHEEP
RREEEEEE!
NO TIME... AND NO GLIDER...

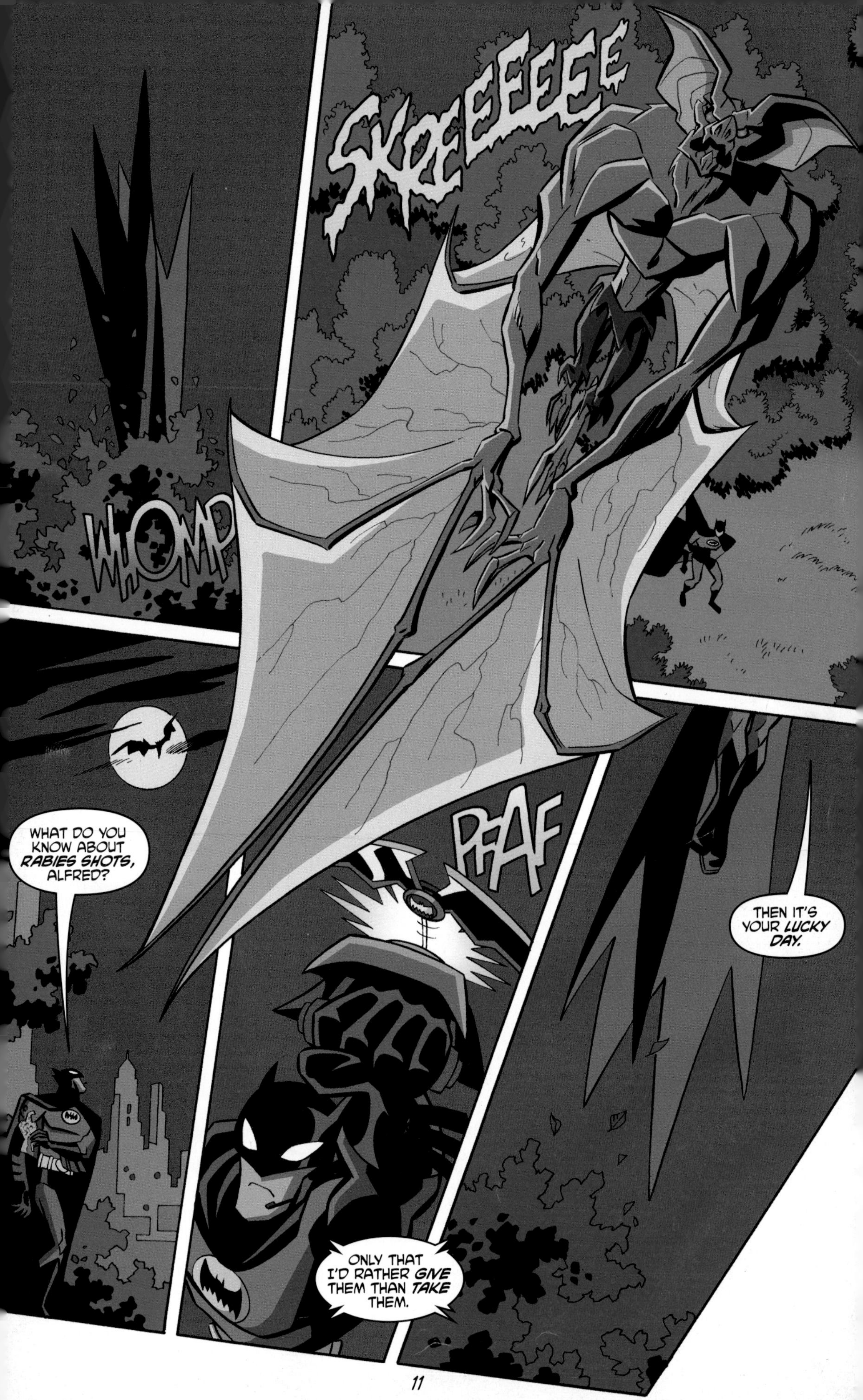
SKREEEEEE
WHOMP
WHAT DO YOU KNOW ABOUT *RABIES SHOTS*, ALFRED?
PFAF
ONLY THAT I'D RATHER *GIVE* THEM THAN *TAKE* THEM.
THEN IT'S YOUR *LUCKY DAY.*

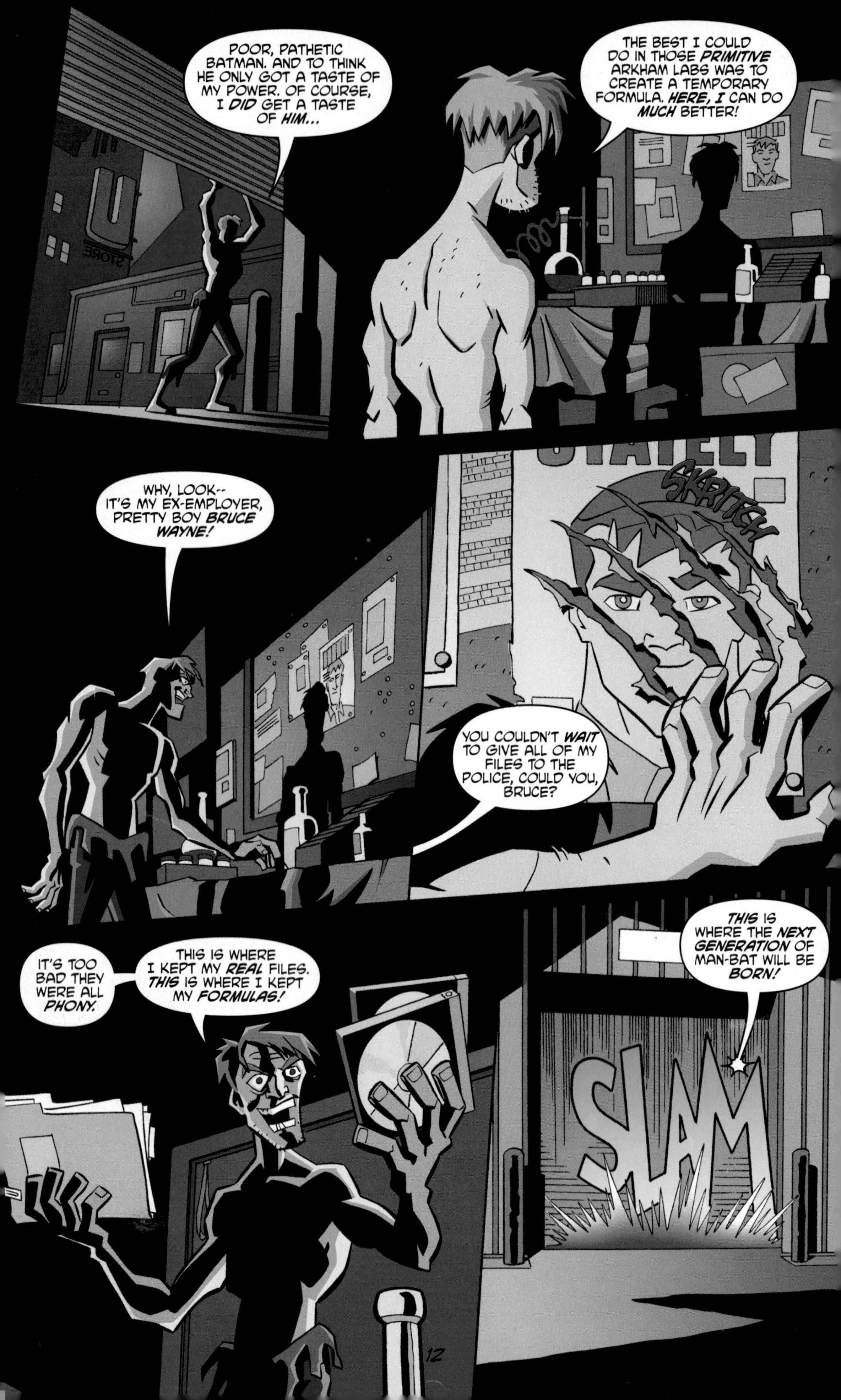
POOR, PATHETIC BATMAN. AND TO THINK HE ONLY GOT A TASTE OF MY POWER. OF COURSE, I *DID* GET A TASTE OF *HIM*...
THE BEST I COULD DO IN THOSE *PRIMITIVE* ARKHAM LABS WAS TO CREATE A TEMPORARY FORMULA. *HERE, I* CAN DO *MUCH* BETTER!
STORE
STATELY
SKRITCH
WHY, LOOK-- IT'S MY EX-EMPLOYER, PRETTY BOY *BRUCE WAYNE!*
YOU COULDN'T *WAIT* TO GIVE ALL OF MY FILES TO THE POLICE, COULD YOU, BRUCE?
IT'S TOO BAD THEY WERE ALL *PHONY.*
THIS IS WHERE I KEPT MY *REAL* FILES. *THIS* IS WHERE I KEPT MY *FORMULAS!*
THIS IS WHERE THE *NEXT GENERATION* OF MAN-BAT WILL BE *BORN!*
SLAM

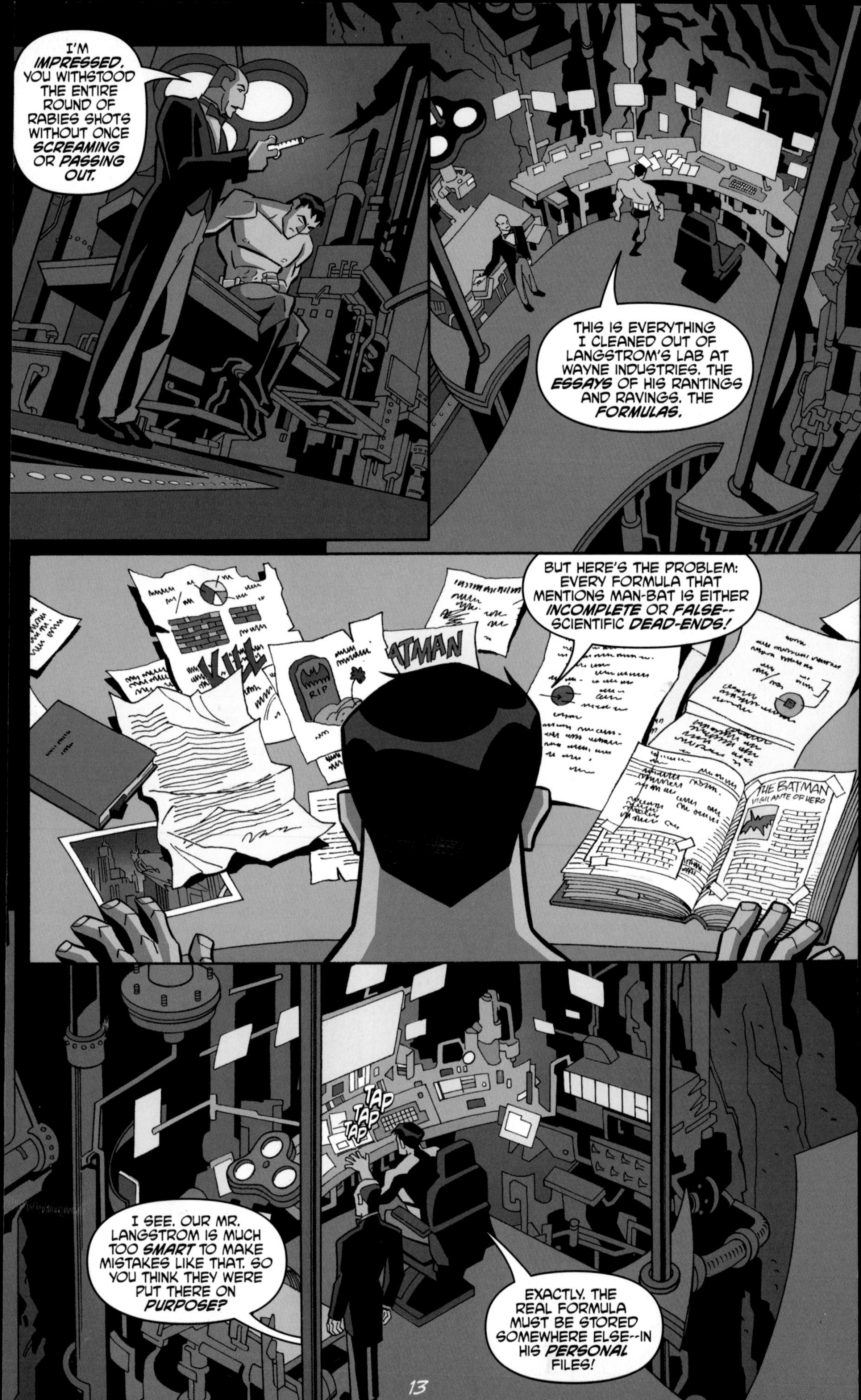
I'M IMPRESSED. YOU WITHSTOOD THE ENTIRE ROUND OF RABIES SHOTS WITHOUT ONCE SCREAMING OR PASSING OUT.
THIS IS EVERYTHING I CLEANED OUT OF LANGSTROM'S LAB AT WAYNE INDUSTRIES. THE ESSAYS OF HIS RANTINGS AND RAVINGS. THE FORMULAS.
BUT HERE'S THE PROBLEM: EVERY FORMULA THAT MENTIONS MAN-BAT IS EITHER INCOMPLETE OR FALSE-- SCIENTIFIC DEAD-ENDS!
THE BATMAN
VIGILANTE OR HERO
TAP TAP TAP
I SEE. OUR MR. LANGSTROM IS MUCH TOO SMART TO MAKE MISTAKES LIKE THAT. SO YOU THINK THEY WERE PUT THERE ON PURPOSE?
EXACTLY. THE REAL FORMULA MUST BE STORED SOMEWHERE ELSE--IN HIS PERSONAL FILES!

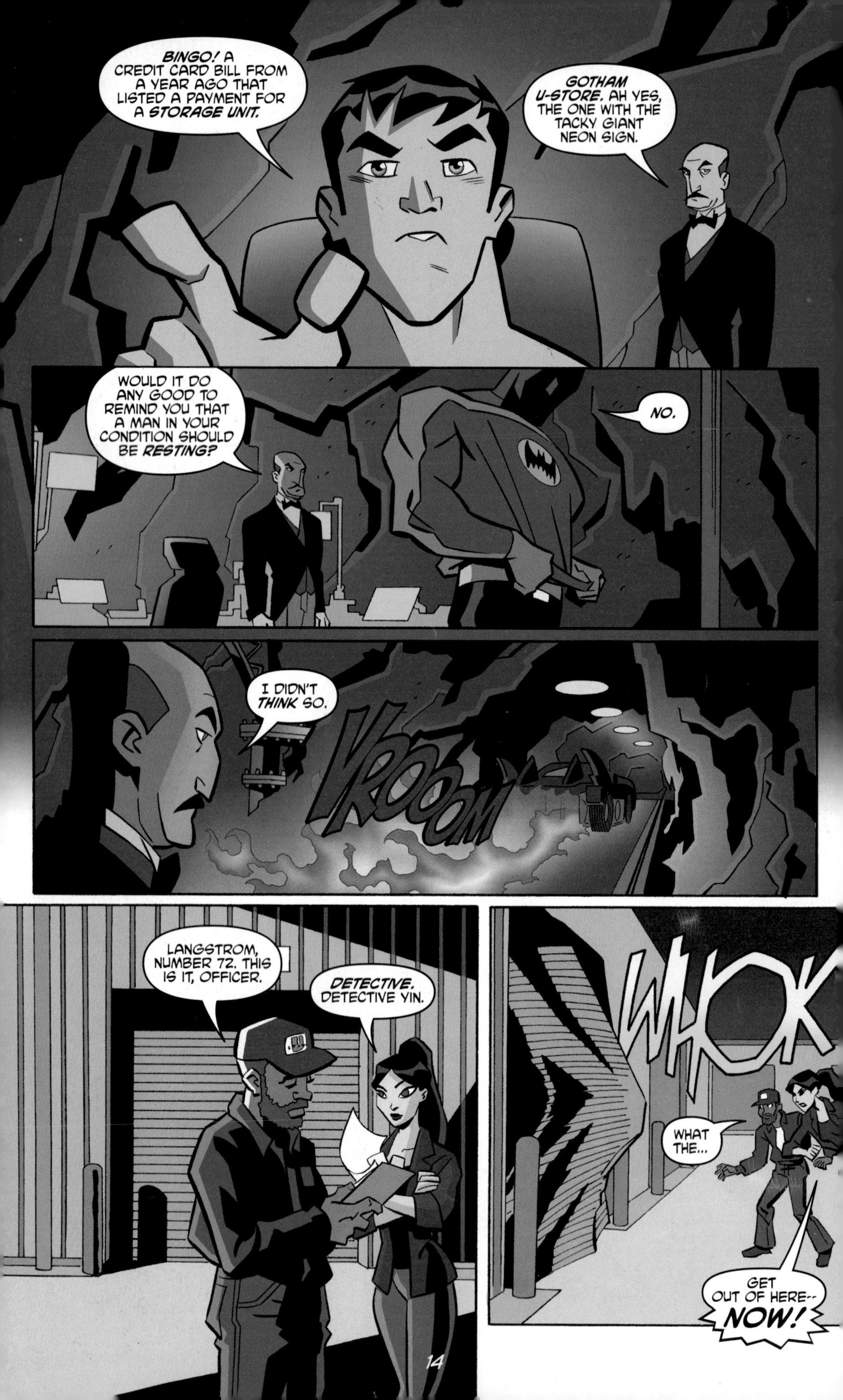
BINGO! A CREDIT CARD BILL FROM A YEAR AGO THAT LISTED A PAYMENT FOR A STORAGE UNIT.
GOTHAM U-STORE. AH YES, THE ONE WITH THE TACKY GIANT NEON SIGN.
WOULD IT DO ANY GOOD TO REMIND YOU THAT A MAN IN YOUR CONDITION SHOULD BE RESTING?
NO.
I DIDN'T THINK SO.
VROOOM
LANGSTROM, NUMBER 72. THIS IS IT, OFFICER.
DETECTIVE. DETECTIVE YIN.
WHOK
WHAT THE...
GET OUT OF HERE-- NOW!

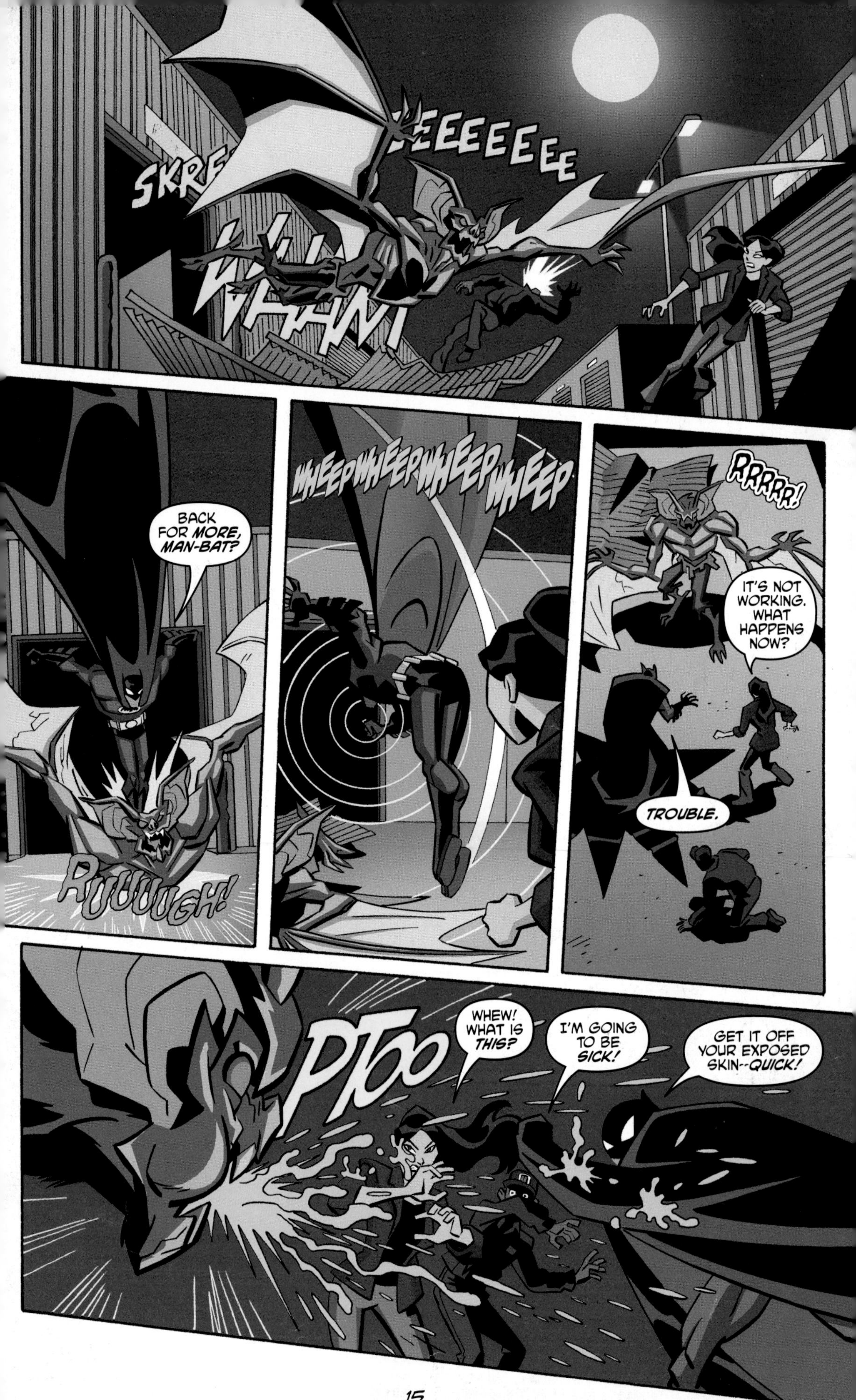
SKREEEEEEEEE
WHAM
BACK FOR MORE, MAN-BAT?
RUUUUGH!
WHEEPWHEEPWHEEPWHEEP
RRRRR!
IT'S NOT WORKING. WHAT HAPPENS NOW?
TROUBLE.
PTOO
WHEW! WHAT IS THIS?
I'M GOING TO BE SICK!
GET IT OFF YOUR EXPOSED SKIN--QUICK!

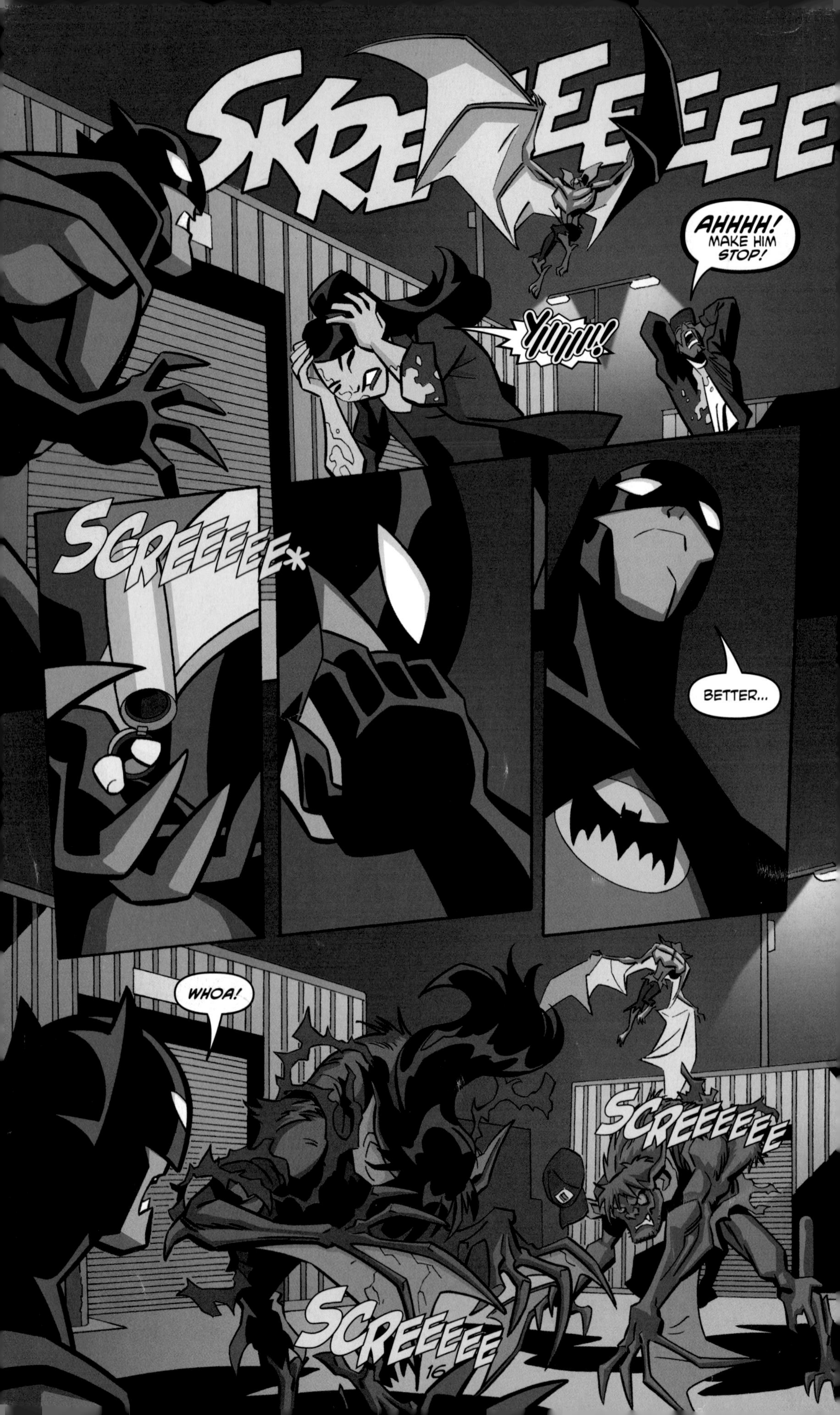
SKREEEEEEEE
AHHHH! MAKE HIM STOP!
YIIIII!
SCREEEEEE*
BETTER...
WHOA!
SCREEEEEEE
SCREEEEEE

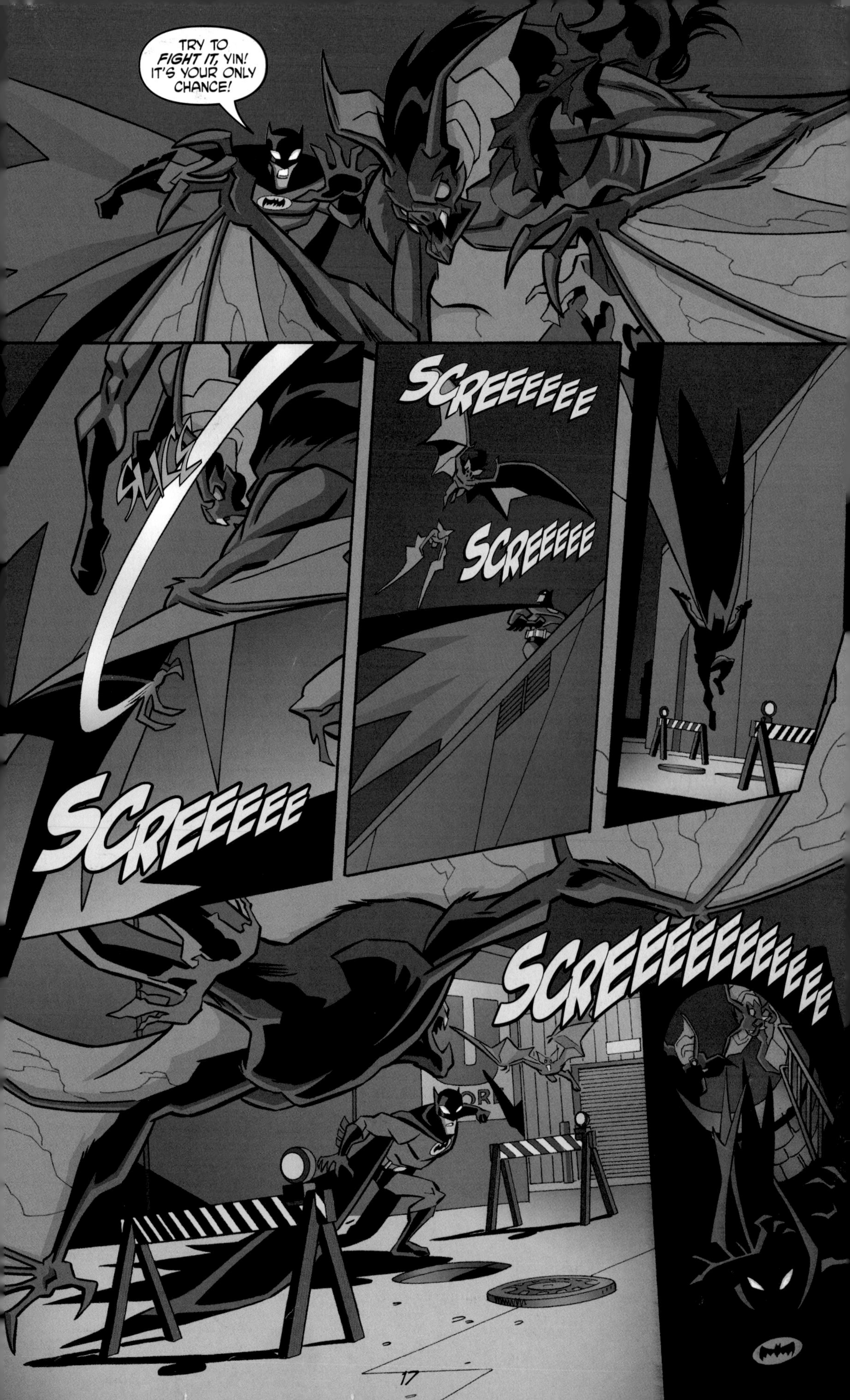
TRY TO *FIGHT IT,* YIN! IT'S YOUR ONLY CHANCE!
SCREEEEEEE
SCREEEEEEE
SCREEEEE
SCREEEEEEEEEEEEE

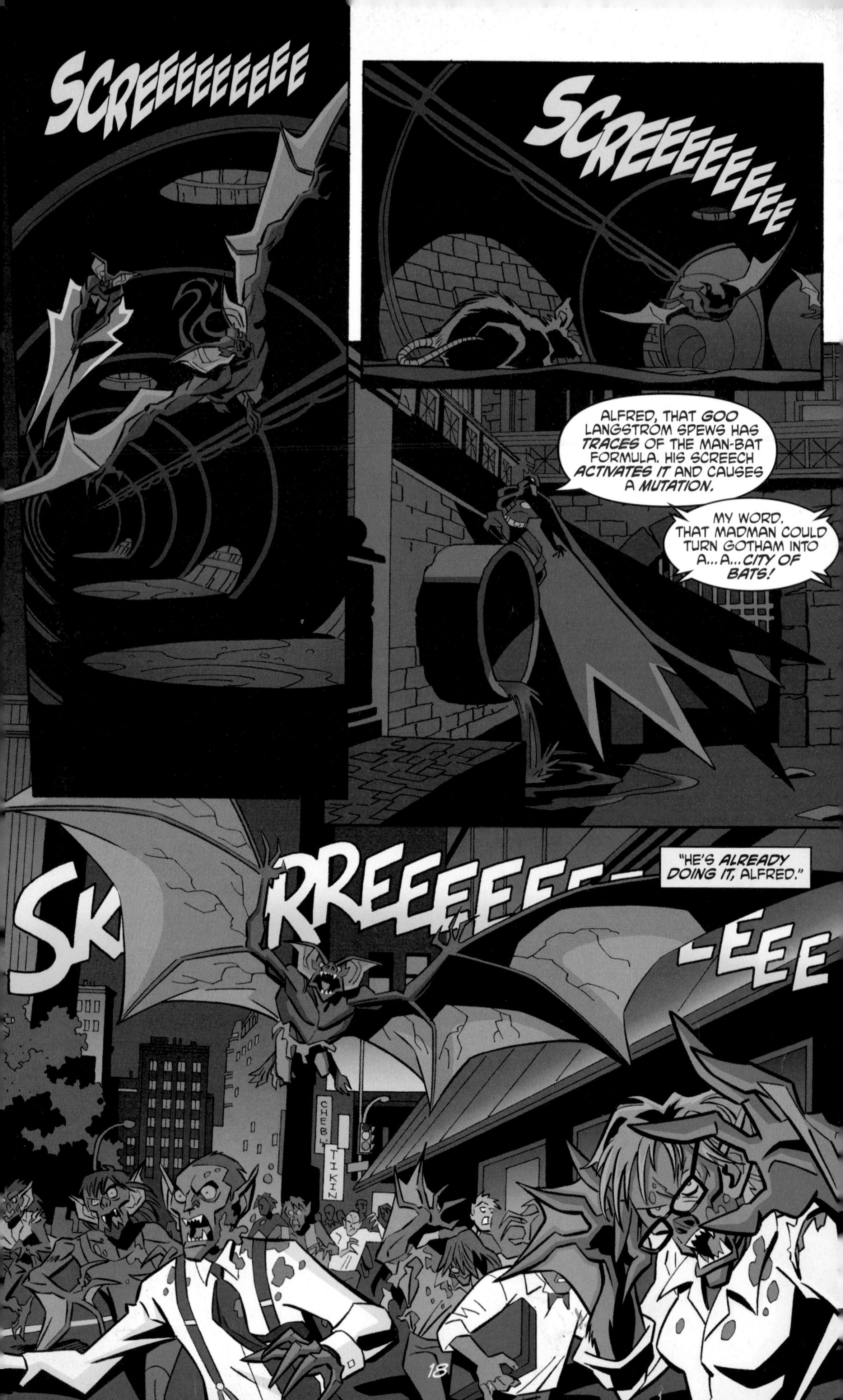
SCREEEEEEEEE
SCREEEEEEEEE
ALFRED, THAT GOO LANGSTROM SPEWS HAS TRACES OF THE MAN-BAT FORMULA. HIS SCREECH ACTIVATES IT AND CAUSES A MUTATION.
MY WORD. THAT MADMAN COULD TURN GOTHAM INTO A... A... CITY OF BATS!
"HE'S ALREADY DOING IT, ALFRED."
SKRREEEEEE--EEEE
CHEBY
TIKIN

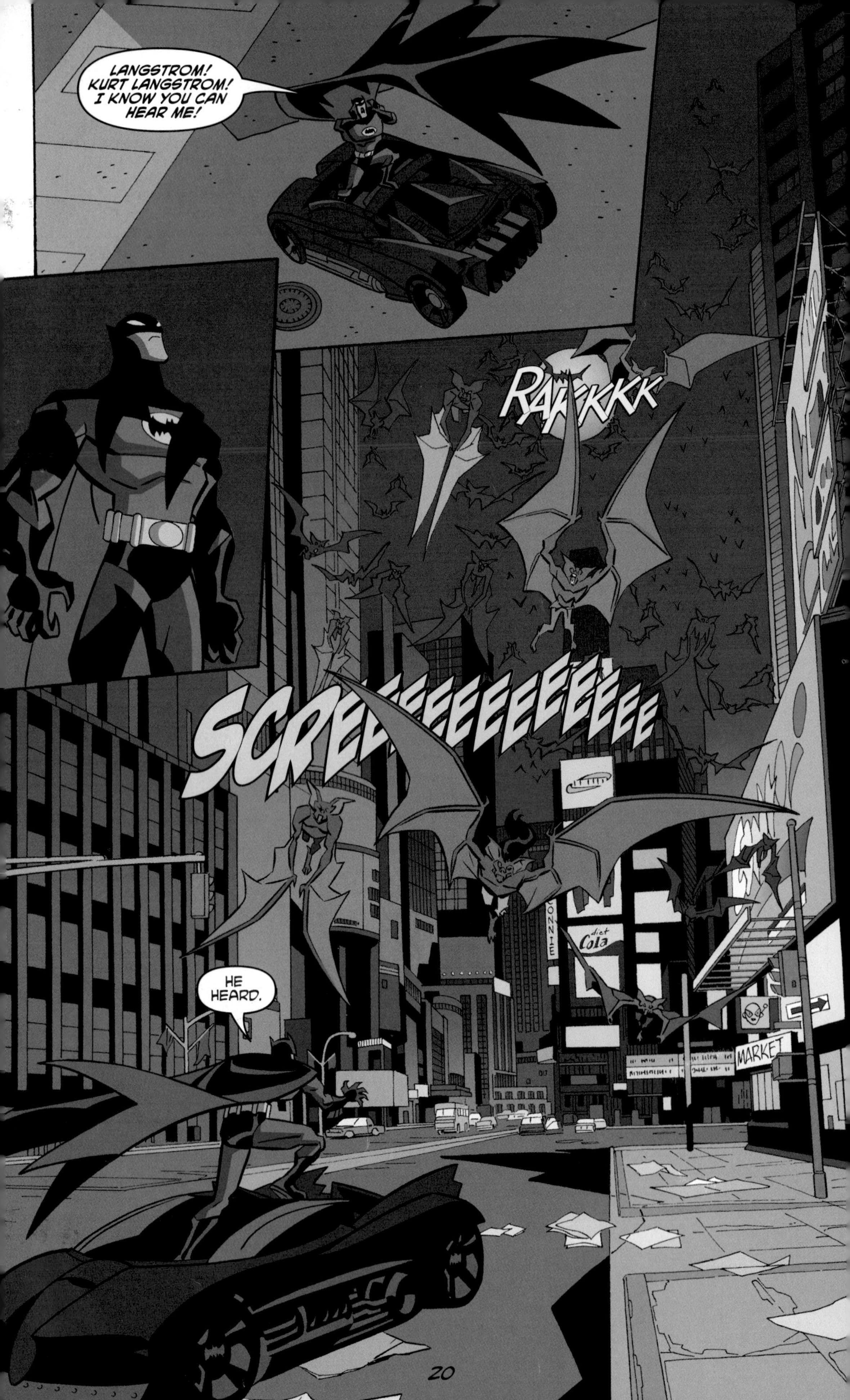
LANGSTROM! KURT LANGSTROM! I KNOW YOU CAN HEAR ME!
RAKKKK
SCREEEEEEEEEEEE
HE HEARD.
diet Cola
CONNIE
MARKET

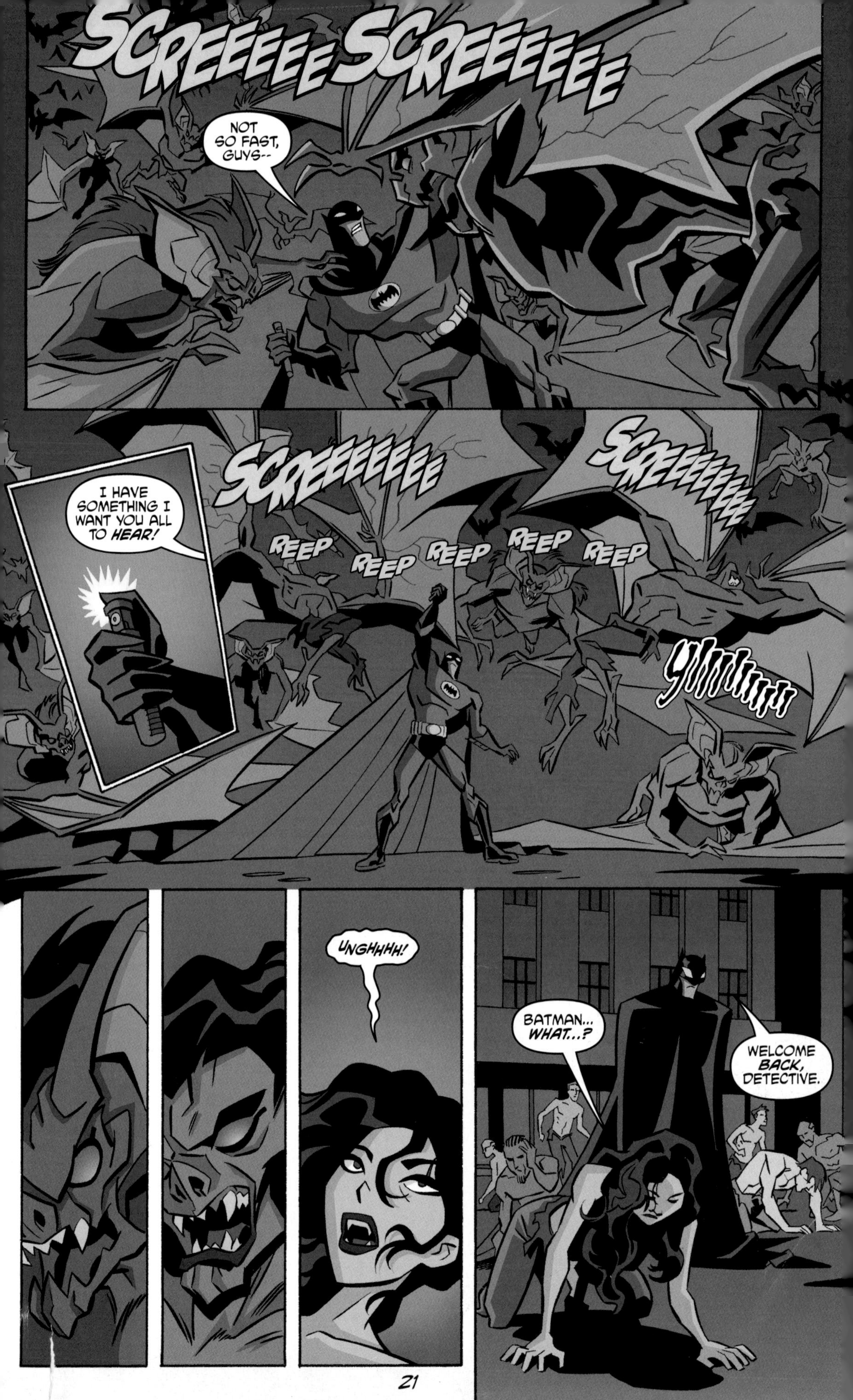
SCREEEEEE SCREEEEEEE
NOT SO FAST, GUYS--
SCREEEEEEEE
SCREEEEEEEEE
I HAVE SOMETHING I WANT YOU ALL TO HEAR!
REEP
REEP
REEP
REEP
REEP
UNGHHHH!
BATMAN... WHAT...?
WELCOME BACK, DETECTIVE.

CREATORS

BILL MATHENY WRITER

Along with comics such as THE BATMAN STRIKES, Bill Matheny has written for TV series including KRYPTO THE SUPERDOG, WHERE'S WALDO, A PUP NAMED SCOOBY-DOO, and many others.

CHRISTOPHER JONES PENCILLER

Christopher Jones is an artist who has worked for DC Comics, Image, Malibu, Caliber, and Sundragon Comics.

TERRY BEATTY INKER

Terry Beatty has inked THE BATMAN STRIKES! and BATMAN: THE BRAVE AND THE BOLD as well as several other DC Comics graphic novels.

GLOSSARY

catastrophic disastrous and destructive

formula rule in science and maths that is written with numbers and symbols

insulated covered with material that stops heat or electricity from entering or escaping

mutation genetic change

nosy someone who is nosy is too interested in things that do not concern them

pathetic feeble or useless

primitive very simple or having to do with an early stage of development

rabies virus that attacks the brain and spinal cord and is spread by the bite of an infected animal

relief feeling of freedom from discomfort, or help given to people in need

vial small glass container used for holding liquids

vigilantes individuals who take the law into their own hands

voltage force of an electrical current as expressed in volts

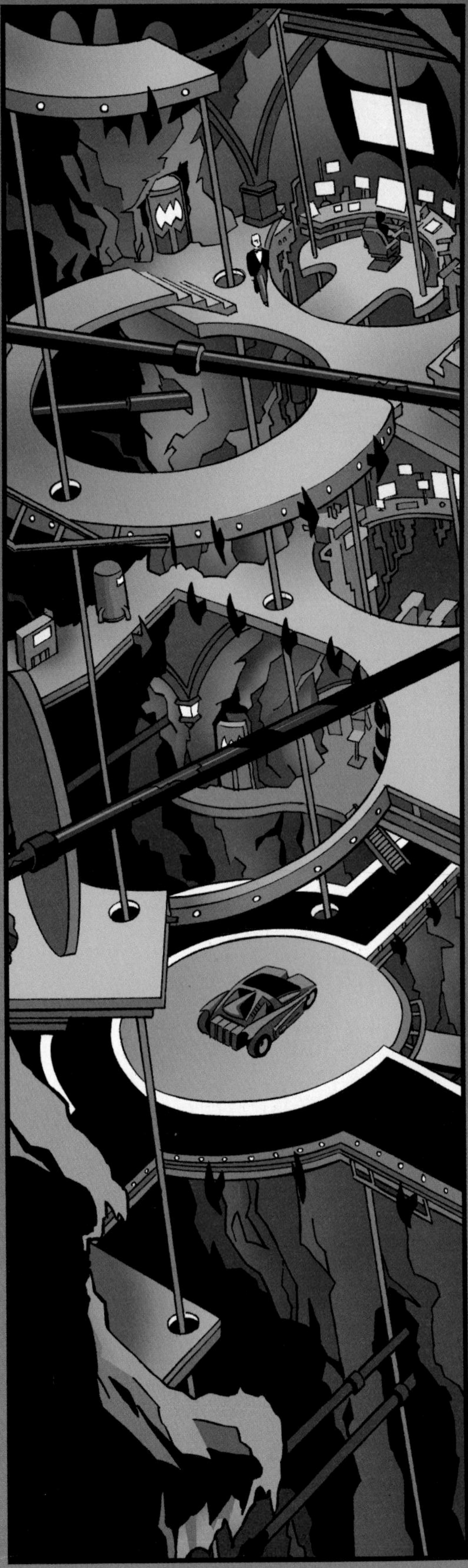

VISUAL QUESTIONS & PROMPTS

1. What do the circular lines around Batman's fist mean? [Hint: they are related to the sound effect at the top of the panel.]

2. Why is the text in the two speech bubbles in the left panel smaller than the normal ones?

4. In the panel at the top right, we see the Man Bat's wings overlapping the panel borders. Why do you think the artists did this? How does the effect make you feel when you read this spread?

3. Batman's Utility Belt is filled with useful gadgets. Make a list of some other items that Batman might keep inside, and explain how they'd help him fight crime.

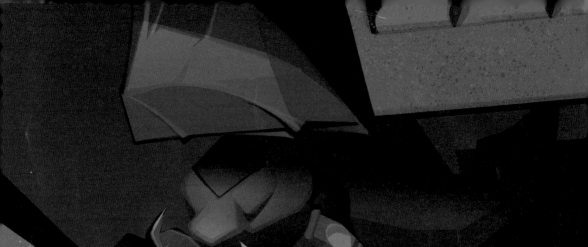

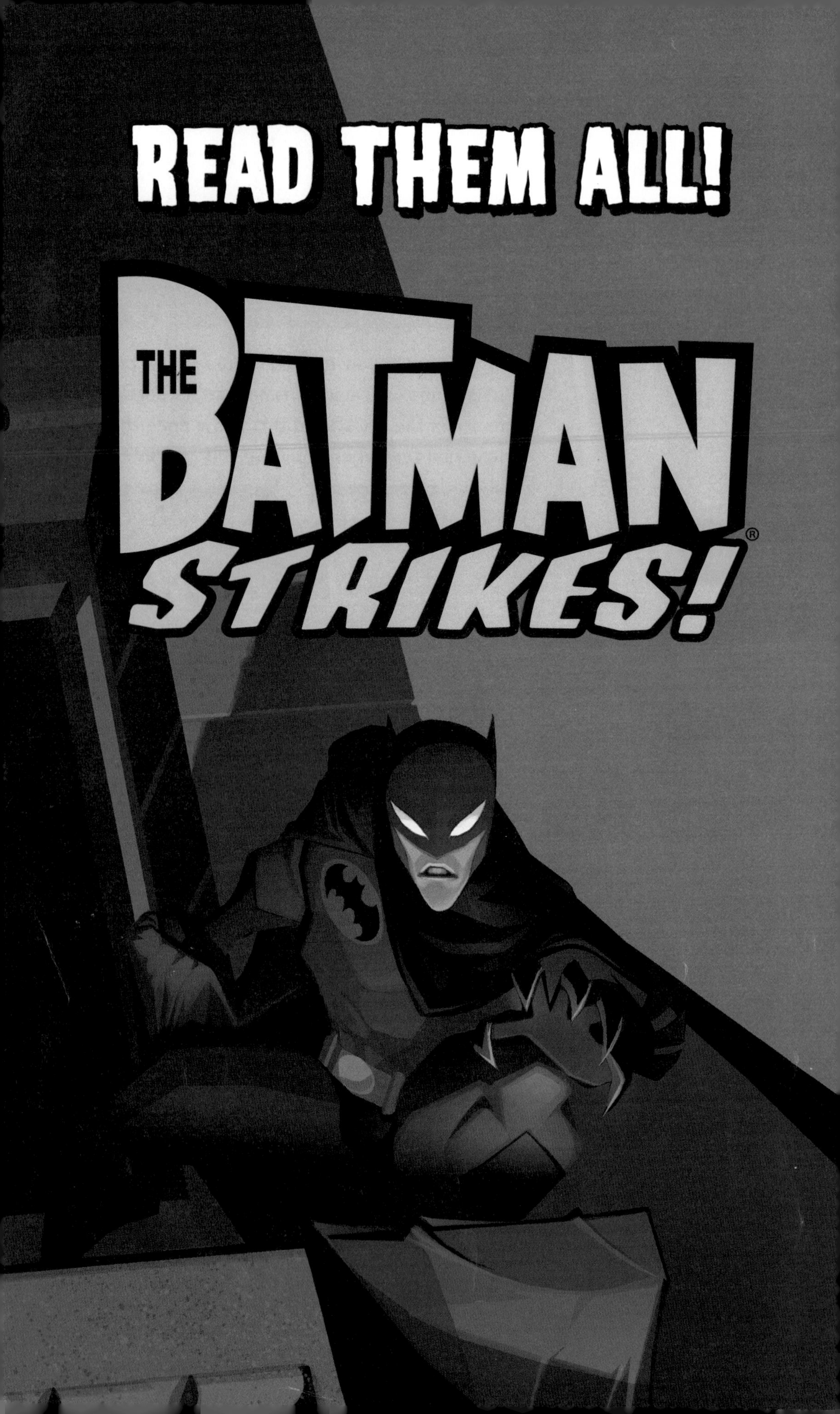

THE BATMAN STRIKES!

READ THEM ALL!